ZEN

禅

The two major religions in Japan are Shintoism and Buddhism. People who practice *Zen* Buddhism try to live a simple and disciplined life that is in harmony with nature. But the ideas of *Zen* have been influential beyond religion. Think of this *Zen* rock garden as our world on a simple scale: the raked gravel represents the ocean, the rocks continents. Then think of how a piece of fabric can be simply decorated, cut and stitched to create a *kimono* that is a national treasure. Or how the act of serving tea can be transformed with grace and precision into a performance. Beauty in simplicity is at the heart of Japanese culture.

YEN 円

Japanese money comes in 1, 5, 10, 50, 100 and 500 *yen* coins, and in 500, 1,000, 5,000 and 10,000 *yen* bills. The bills are very colorful, with pictures of famous people like scholars or writers. The blank areas are pictures in the paper called watermarks that you can see when they are held up to the light. The amount of *yen* you can buy with one United States dollar changes all the time. In 1971, one dollar was worth about 300 *yen*—by 1991, one dollar was worth only about 125 *yen*.

WOKUMAN

ウォークマン

A Japanese company called Sony invented the compact tape player and light-weight headphones that go everywhere. To name it, they made up the word "Walkman," which in Japanese is pronounced *Wokuman.* Before they introduced it in the United States, they were told: "You can't call it Walkman; it's not proper English." But many people had already heard about the tiny tape players and wanted to buy a "Walkman." So Walkman it was.

UKIYO-E

Beautiful prints like this famous picture of Mount Fuji are printed from woodblocks and are called *ukiyo-e*, "oo-kee-oh-eh." It takes four master craftsmen to make *ukiyo-e*: the Artist who draws the picture, the Woodcarver who cuts the image into one block of wood for each color, the Papermaker who makes the paper by hand, and finally the Printer who mixes the inks, paints them onto the woodblocks, and prints them one by one onto the paper.

浮世絵

TANGO NO SEKKU 端午の節句

There are many festival days in Japan and some of the most colorful are for children. For centuries Boys Day, *Tango no Sekku*, was celebrated May 5th, but it is now considered Children's Day. Families fly carp streamers in their gardens and display warrior dolls in their homes. Girls Day or the Doll Festival, *Momo no Sekku*, is celebrated March 3rd. On November 15th, *Shichigosan*, parents take children who are 7, 5, or 3 to shrines to give thanks that their children have reached these ages.

SUSHI

is raw or slightly cooked seafood like tuna, salmon, sea urchin, or octopus that is carefully made into small portions with vinegar-flavored rice and vegetables. *Sushi* can be shaped by hand, molded in a small box, or rolled in dried seaweed. You eat *sushi* with chopsticks or your fingers, barely dipping each piece into soy sauce with a little horseradish in it, then savoring the sweet taste. Isn't this plate of *sushi* beautiful? For a *sushi* chef, the way a meal looks is almost as important as how it tastes.

寿司

RANDOSERU

As a child in Japan, your *randoseru* or knapsack follows you through school. It has compartments for books, pencils, and lunch. These little girls are probably six and just starting first grade. After several years their *randoseru* will be battered and worn, a sign they are good students and carry lots of books between home and school. Knapsacks were introduced into Japan by the Dutch, and *randoseru* is how the Japanese pronounce the Dutch word for knapsack, "ransel."

ランドセル

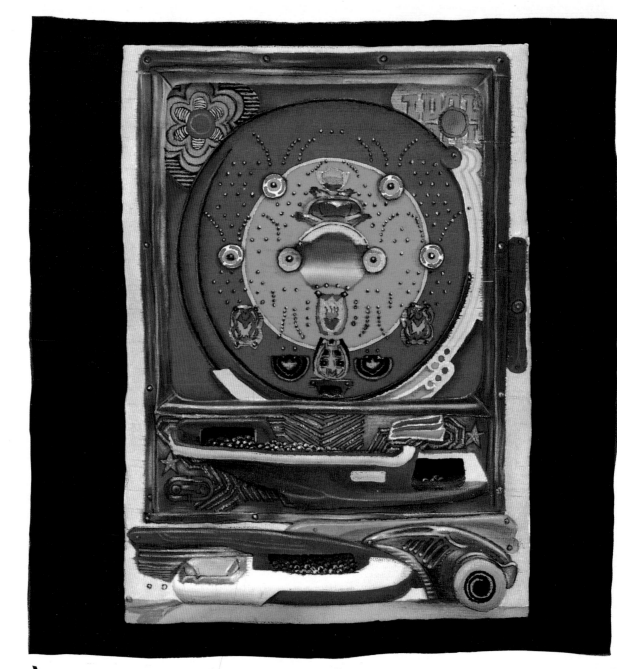

PACHINKO

Pachinko is a pinball game with small steel balls that the player tries to sink into holes in a brightly colored vertical board. The name comes from the word *pachin* which describes the sound the balls make when the game is played. You might have a toy *pachinko* at home, but only adults can go into *pachinko* parlors where they play to win small prizes. Millions of Japanese play *pachinko* every day.

パチンコ

ORIGAMI

More than 600 years ago Japanese children were folding squares of colored paper into cranes, frogs, helmets, and birds. The most common *origami* shape is the crane. If you have a wish you might want to make a thousand cranes, or *sembazuru*, to help make your wish come true. Many *sembazuru* hang in the Peace Park in Hiroshima, because the crane is also a symbol of long life. *Origami* is used in Japanese schools to teach dexterity, precision, and basic concepts of geometry.

折り紙

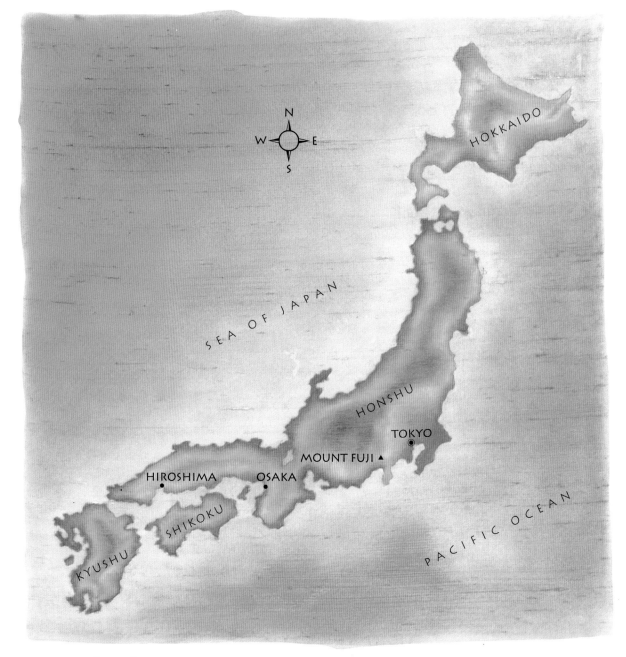

NIPPON

Millions of years ago undersea volcanoes erupted and formed the string of islands 1,200 miles long that we know as Japan—or *Nippon*. Almost two-thirds of Japan is mountainous, and it has frequent earthquakes and occasional volcanic eruptions. Japanese schoolchildren have earthquake drills just as you have fire drills. It's about the same size as California, but Japan has about half as many people as the United States. Most of them live in big cities like *Tokyo* or *Osaka*. The climate is similar to the eastern coast of the United States—colder in the north, hot in the south.

日本

HIRAGANA   KATAKANA   KANJI   EARLY CHINESE CHARACTERS   ANCIENT PICTOGRAPHS

MOJI means system of writing. In the middle column above the *kanji* characters for "sun" and "root" or "origin" are combined to make *Nippon*, which means the land of the rising sun, or Japan. *Kanji* are Chinese characters which are based on pictographs. Only about 2,000 *kanji* are used regularly, but there are over 45,000 in a complete dictionary. To the left of the *kanji* are the sounds for *Nippon* in two phonetic alphabets: *hiragana* for Japanese words, and *katakana* for words borrowed from Western languages. *Kanji*, *hiragana*, and *katakana* are all used in Japanese writing, sometimes in the same sentence.

文字

KIMONO

Japanese once wore *kimonos* every day, just as you wear jeans or skirts and blouses. Today children wear *kimonos* only on festival days. Whether they are made from silk or ordinary cotton, most *kimonos* are decorated—with painting, tie dyeing and intricate stitchery. They are always made from a single length of cloth 14 inches wide, that is first decorated and then cut into eight rectangular panels without waste and stitched together with straight seams. Some *kimonos* are so beautiful they are considered national treasures.

着
物

JANKEN

Have you ever played the game rock, scissors, paper? Japanese children do too. They call it *janken* and when they play they call out, *"Jan, ken, pon."* Sometimes it's the same game American children play, but other times it's a way to decide whose turn is next, sort of like "Eenie, meenie, minie, moe." The name comes from the word *ken*, which means fist.

じゃんけん

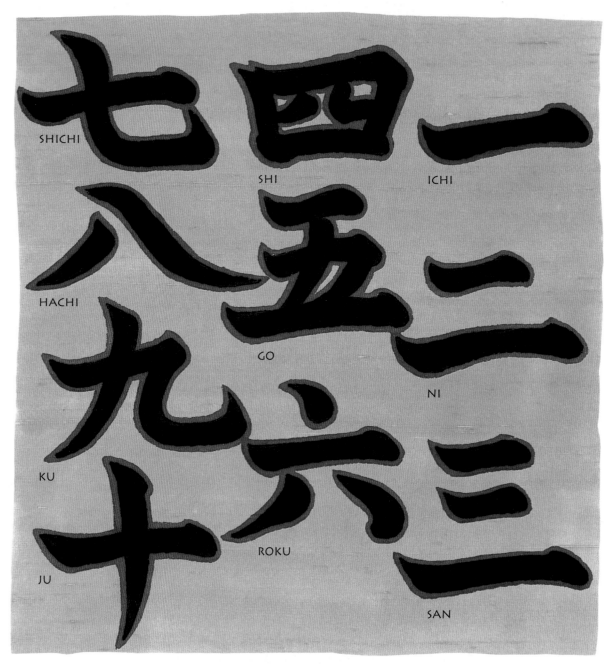

七 SHICHI

八 HACHI

九 KU

十 JU

四 SHI

五 GO

六 ROKU

一 ICHI

二 NI

三 SAN

ICHINISAN

literally means "one two three," or counting. You can learn to count from one to ten in Japanese. Begin at the upper right hand corner and read from top to bottom, right to left. "Ee-chee" is how you pronounce 1, "nee" 2, "sahn" 3, "shee" 4, "go" 5, "ro-koo" 6, "shi-chee" 7, "hah-chee" 8, "koo" 9, and "joo" 10. Japanese characters are often based on ancient symbols called pictographs. Can you see where one, two, and three come from?

一
二
三

HIROSHIMA

The war between Japan and the United States 広島 began when the Japanese attacked Pearl Harbor on December 7, 1941. On August 6, 1945 the United States dropped an atomic bomb on the city of *Hiroshima*, and within days the Japanese surrendered. Almost 90,000 people died in the explosion and even today some people suffer from diseases caused by the radiation. A Peace Park was created in *Hiroshima* and each year on August 6th people float lanterns past the Atomic Dome to remember those who died and pray for lasting peace.

GENKAN

The small entryway between the street and the main living room is 玄関 the *genkan*. To keep the *tatami* clean, when you come into the house leave your shoes in the *genkan*, but turn them toward the street so you can slip into them easily when you go out. The sliding panels are made of paper pasted on wooden frames and can be moved to make the rooms larger or smaller.

FUTON

Japan's cities are crowded and every bit of space must be used as efficiently as possible. In a traditional Japanese home, one room is used for many purposes such as living, dining, and sleeping. You sleep on a thick cotton pad or *futon*, which is folded up in the morning and stored in a closet until bedtime. The floors are covered with woven straw mats called *tatami,* and instead of chairs there are cushions on the *tatami*.

ふとん

ETO

Are you clever? Perhaps you were born in the year of the monkey. *Eto* is the Japanese zodiac, which originated in ancient China. It is based on 12 animals (rat, ox, tiger, hare, dragon, snake, horse, ram, monkey, rooster, dog, and boar) and 5 elements (wood, fire, earth, metal, and water) combined to create a cycle of 60 years. Often arranged in a circle, they also indicate time and direction. The rat, for instance, points north and stands for the two hours around midnight. Some people believe they take on characteristics of the animal of their birth year.

干支

DARUMA

The next time you have a goal, perhaps to do well on a test, you may want to buy a *daruma* doll. They are made from papier-mâché and come in many sizes, always without eyes. You paint in one of the eyes to indicate you have a goal. When you reach your goal, paint in the other eye. If you have another goal, you need a new *daruma*. The shape of the fat dolls comes from Bodai Daruma, the founder of *Zen* Buddhism in China, who is said to have meditated so long that he lost the use of his arms and legs.

だるま

CHANOYU

There was a time when *chanoyu*, the tea ceremony, was performed only by *Zen* priests and *samurai* warriors, but now anyone can study it. *Chanoyu* often takes place in a small building apart from the house, so it is a way to escape the problems of daily life. And *chanoyu* is so steeped in tradition—how the room is decorated, the artful movements of the person who prepares and serves the tea, even how the dishes are cleaned and put away—that the ceremony is also a performance.

茶の湯

BUNRAKU

A night at the *bunraku* puppet theater is a dramatic trip back 文楽 in time. The puppets are half-life-size wooden dolls operated by three men: the master puppeteer moves the doll's head, eyelids, eyeballs, eyebrows, mouth, and right hand; a second moves only the left hand, and a third moves the feet. A chanter tells the story, playing all the parts. The stories are so compelling and the puppeteers and chanter so skillful, that you forget these are dolls and are soon caught up in their struggles to be honorable people.

AIKIDO

合気道

Imagine that you know every move your opponent is going to make. Now imagine your opponent pushing you. Don't push back, pull him toward you—he will fall forward and you will be in control! This is *aikido*: keeping your mind open to anticipate your opponent's moves, then using his own moves against him. *Aikido* comes from martial arts that are over 1,000 years old and were practiced by highly trained warriors. Now it is practiced all over the world by ordinary men and women and even children.

ABOUT THIS BOOK

Even before the first emperor of Japan began his reign in 660 B.C., Japanese culture was well established. Today, this ancient land is one of the most modern countries on Earth, and everywhere you can see the contrast between old and new.

We considered hundreds of concepts, objects, and activities from every area of Japanese life before choosing the 22 topic words. Because the Japanese language has no sounds for the letters L, Q, V and X, there are no topics beginning with these letters. Japanese has only five vowel sounds: a as in ah, i as in machine, u as in moon, e as in met, and o as in no.

Yoshi's pictures were painted with dyes on silk cloth, using the same basic techniques used to decorate *kimonos*. Like many other elements of Japanese culture, these techniques originated in China, and Yoshi studied them when she was an art student in Tokyo. She has modernized her techniques somewhat, but the ancient traditions of the East remain.

Because this book is about an oriental country, we have given it an oriental structure. The pages go from back to front and right to left, like a traditional Japanese book. (Of course, Japanese people would say *our* books go from back to front.) On each page, the topic word is shown in Japanese the way they read, starting at the top right corner and reading down. It is also shown in English the way we read, starting at the top left corner and reading to the right.

We have tried to give you words and images to bring today's Japan closer. Now perhaps your imagination will add the quiet tinkle of temple bells, the sweet taste of *sushi*, the cushion of *tatami* mats under your bare feet, the peace of a *Zen* garden.

A TO ZEN

Ruth Wells

a book of
Japanese
culture

Yoshi

Picture Book Studio

To Melissa and Rob, believers.—R.W.

To my family in Japan:
my parents, Masao and Emiko;
my brother Shinji and his wife Chiaki;
and my nephews, Kaiji and Yō.—Y.

Library of Congress Cataloging-in-Publication Data

Wells, Ruth.

A to Zen: a book of Japanese culture / by Ruth Wells ; illustrated by Yoshi.

p. cm.

Summary: Introduces Japanese words from A to Z.

Book is designed to be read from back to front and from right to left.

ISBN 0-88708-175-4 : $15.95

1. Japanese language—Transliteration into English—Juvenile literature.

[1. Alphabet. 2. Japanese language materials—Bilingual.]

I. Yoshi, ill. II. Title.

PL522.W45 1992

495.6'82421—dc20   91-14183

CIP

AC

Ask yor bookseller for these other *Picture Book Studio* books illustrated by Yoshi:

Magical Hands by Marjorie Barker

Big Al by Andrew Clements

And these books written and illustrated by Yoshi:

1,2,3

The Butterfly Hunt

Who's Hiding Here?